Published by B & F Publishing, Spokane, Washington

Developed in Post Falls, Idaho by Crown Media and Printing, Inc.
www.crownmediacorp.com

Edited by Bonnie Elliott

ISBN# 978-0-9839-4370-9

Cougar Cub Tales
The Sneezy Wheezy Day

Story and Pictures by Sharon Cramer

For Daryl

The cougar cub kittens were sister and brother,

Who lived in their den by the edge of the hills.

They played every day, one with the other

And practiced their pouncing and bouncing cat skills.

The sun peeked so happily over the ridge,

As girl cougar bounded just barely ahead.

"Hurry! We're almost to the stone bridge!"

So, onward the boy and girl cougar sped.

"I can't wait to swim in the crystalline pool,"

The boy cougar panted, now somewhat behind.

"It will be quite refreshing, and wonderfully cool."

Just then, he staggered and started to drool.

"My eyes don't seem right and my tongue feels so thick.

I really don't think I feel very well."

The girl cougar noticed, "You look kinda sick.

But there's someone I know who can probably tell.

He's feathery white and slick as a lick!"

They went to the woods to find the White Owl,

He peered for a bit into boy cougar's eyes.

"Yep... I can see that something's afoul,

You just need a slice of care-berry pie."

So he gobbled one up with a gulp and a growl.

But the boy cougar still continued to lag.

So, girl cougar led him into the trees.

"I think if we speak to the Royal King Stag

He can tell us a cure for a sick, little cub,

Some potion or brew for a cougar disease."

"You've caught a bad bug," the King Stag deduced,

Tilting his head, so regal and wise.

"Tickle your nose with the tail of a goose,

And do it before the next blue-moon rise!"

They thanked him and said their urgent goodbyes.

The Canadian Goose was so happy to help,

And tickled his nose that very same day.

Boy cougar coughed and gave a sad yelp,

"My throat feels like fire, my head stuffed with hay...

Do you think I will ever again be okay?"

"Maybe Red Fox will know what to do."

His sister declared, "Let's give it a try.

She's clever and smart and so very sly.

It's not very far, just a mile or two.

She's certain to know of a treatment for you."

The Fox's intentions were admirably kind,

Although, not really helpful at all.

The boy cougar tried to steady the ball,

But his ears were all stuffy; his balance was poor.

So, time after time it continued to fall.

Girl cougar sat for a moment or two,

"Perhaps, if we go see the Razorback Hog?

He lives by the marble and marmalade cliff."

Brother agreed with a slobbery sniff,

"It's not very far from the burgling bog."

"Plaster your chest with saraphine clay.

Wait till it dries, then jump in the pond."

The Razorback nodded, "Back the same way...

Back on the banks of the burgling bog,

And you'll feel just like new by the end of the day."

After the clay and a dip in the pool,

The cougar cubs dried on the bank in the sun.

Sister was worried. Her brother was sick!

He was starting to fade, and shivering some.

His nose was too warm and had started to run.

Boy cougar sniffled and thought very hard,

"What if we visit the Grizzly Old Bear?"

Girl cougar tried to sound happy and sure,

"Of course! I agree! He may know a cure."

So, off to the cliffs went the cougar-cub pair.

From the back of the cave mused the Grizzly Old Bear.

He looked the boy cougar full up and down.

"The reason you're warm is you have too much hair.

Best if you trim it as short as you dare."

Then, they clipped him all up, from his tail to his crown.

Hair cut complete, the girl cougar said,

"It's really not bad, but how do you feel?"

"Tired—I think maybe ready for bed."

So, the bald little cougar headed downhill.

The day was still warm, but he'd taken a chill.

"I have an idea!" Girl cougar exclaimed,

As she made him a cup of kittycat tea.

"Lay yourself down and make yourself comfy."

She gathered his favorite pillow and blanky,

Then, wrapped him all up, warm as can be!

While boy cougar rested, she gave him a hug.

After just a few hours, he opened his eyes.

"I feel so much better, snug as a bug!"

Then he realized, to his surprise...

It was SIS who had made him feel better today!

Because she had cared...

Every step of the way!

The End

Sharon Jean Cramer is the author and illustrator of the award winning children's picture book series, Cougar Cub Tales. She very much enjoys writing and illustrating children's books. Born in Jamestown, New York in 1960, Sharon has lived throughout the United States, finally settling in the Pacific Northwest. She went to Idaho State University and then Gonzaga University. Sharon is married and has three sons of her own. She and the Cougar Cubs currently reside, happily, in Spokane, Washington.

Other Books by Sharon Cramer
Cougar Cub Tales: Lost and Alone
Cougar Cub Tales: I'm Just Like You
Marlow and the Monster